For my girls - K.B.

The Goblin's Blue Blanket

Kieron Black

shrine bell

www.shrinebell.com

This is Ogie.
Ogie is a goblin.

He lives with his family
in a little goblin village,
high in the mountains of the
faraway island of Goblinia.

Ogie has a cat named Gerald
who is very annoying.
He also has a blue blanket.

Ogie is **very** fond of Gerald,
but he **loves** his blue blanket.

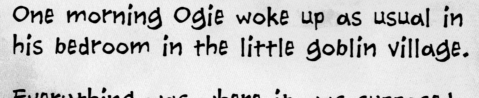

One morning Ogie woke up as usual in his bedroom in the little goblin village.

Everything was where it was supposed to be: his creatures were there, the friends of his creatures were there, and their friends were there too.

Everything was there, except for his blue blanket.

'My blanket!' wailed Ogie.
'It's GONE!'

'Oh – my – go – blin!' gasped Ogie's mum. 'What HAS happened to your room?'

But Ogie wasn't listening. 'We have to find it!' he cried.

So they looked. But they couldn't find it **anywhere**. It was **definitely** lost.

'It can't be far,' said Mum. 'Why don't you go and ask your dad? Maybe he saw it before he went out this morning?'

Ogie found Dad hard at work.
No one knew what Dad **actually** did,
but everyone knew he was **very** good at it.

'Hello son,' he said. 'You're just in time. Climb up and let's see how this thing works!'

'No thanks,' replied Ogie. 'Dad, have you seen my blue blanket?'

'Sorry, no,' said Dad. 'Maybe your grandad has? He's up the mountain now, you could go and ask him?'

'Hello Ogie,' Grandad called,
'and hello Gerald! Are you
two coming snowboarding?'

'No thanks. Grandad; have you seen my blue blanket?'

'No, sorry,' said Grandad. 'Don't worry though; I'm **always** losing things! Remember when I lost Grandma?'

'Yep!' Ogie laughed. 'But she turned up in the end!'

'Exactly!' said Grandad. 'You could ask your sister if she has seen your blanket?'

'Hey Ogie!' called Zamzam, who was feeding her pets. 'Come and help me, it's Noodle-Tuesday! Gerald can share, too!'

'Have you seen my blanket?' shouted up Ogie.

'The blue one?' asked Zamzam.

'Yes,' Ogie said, 'the blue one.'

'The **smelly** blue one, full of holes?' she asked.

'YES,' Ogie said, 'the **smelly** blue one, full of holes!'

'Nope. Sorry!' Zamzam replied. 'Maybe Bogie has, he's at the skate park.'

'Hey Ogie! Hey Gerald!' shouted Ogie's brother Bogie. 'Come and join us! But where are your skateboards?'

'We're looking for my blue blanket,' said Ogie grumpily. 'Have **you** seen it?'

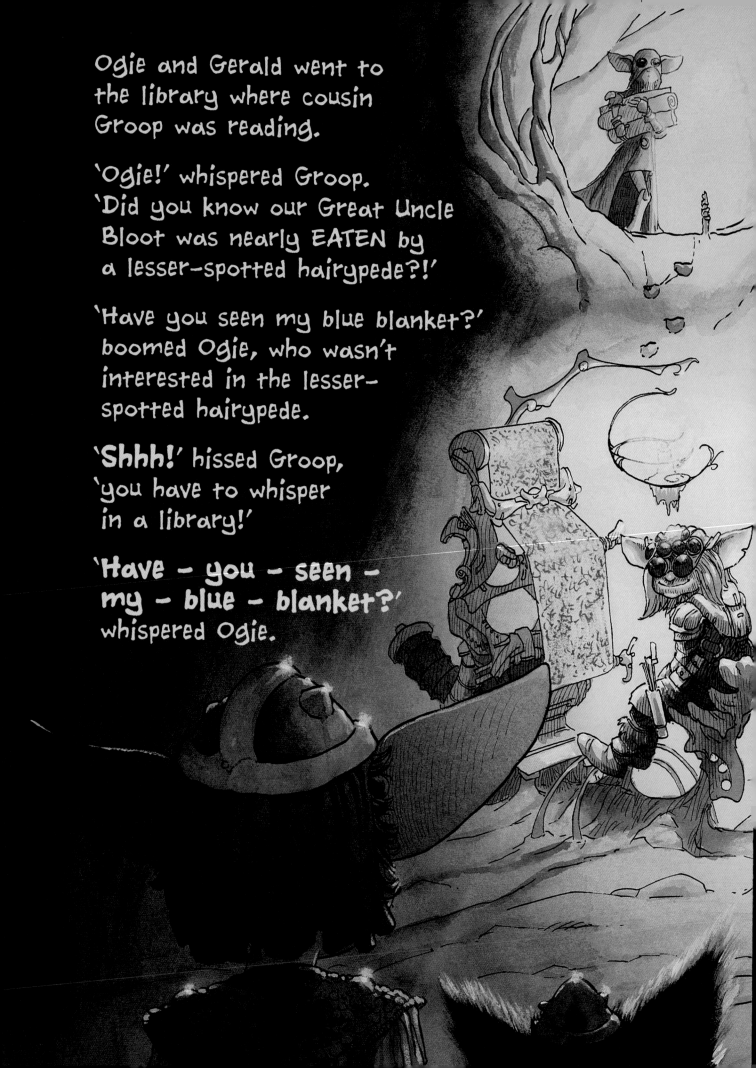

Ogie and Gerald went to the library where cousin Groop was reading.

'Ogie!' whispered Groop. 'Did you know our Great Uncle Bloot was nearly EATEN by a lesser-spotted hairypede?!'

'Have you seen my blue blanket?' boomed Ogie, who wasn't interested in the lesser-spotted hairypede.

'**Shhh!**' hissed Groop, 'you have to whisper in a library!'

'**Have – you – seen – my – blue – blanket?**' whispered Ogie.

'Sorry, no,' replied Groop,
'have you asked the dragon trainers?'

But Toog Grimple the dragon trainer hadn't seen Ogie's blue blanket.

You missed a bit...

And Jeek the troll washer hadn't seen Ogie's blue blanket ...

They **didn't** find it hanging off a tree in the Slimewoods ...

They **didn't** find it sinking in the Goblinian Jam Pits ...

'Meep,'
shrugged Gerald.

'You're right,'
replied Ogie,
'let's go home.
But ... '

'Oh Gerald. Where **is** it?'

Back at home, Ogie told Mum about their day.

'It's OK,' she said. 'Sometimes when you lose something it turns up, like Grandma did, and sometimes it doesn't.'

'But missing something doesn't have to mean **missing out** – like you did today because you were upset. That was a shame, wasn't it?'

'Yes, it was,' said Ogie quietly.

'If someone **has** found your blanket,' said Mum,
'it might make them just as happy as it made you.'

'I like that idea,' replied Ogie.

'That's my goblin!' said Mum. 'And anyway,
I found your old red blanket, will that do for now?'

'Maybe ... ' sniffed Ogie with half a smile.

And you know what?

The red blanket did **just** fine.

And the smelly blue one,
full of holes?

It made someone **very** happy indeed!

The Goblin's Blue Blanket

Kieron Black

First published in 2019 by Shrine Bell, an imprint of Vertebrate Publishing.

Shrine Bell
Crescent House, 228 Psalter Lane, Sheffield, S11 8UT, United Kingdom.
www.shrinebell.com

A CIP catalogue record for this book is available from the British Library.

ISBN 978-1-911342-87-8 (Paperback)

10 9 8 7 6 5 4 3 2 1

Production by Vertebrate Publishing.
www.v-publishing.co.uk

Shrine Bell and Vertebrate Publishing are committed to printing on paper from sustainable sources.

FSC
MIX
Paper from responsible sources
FSC® C016973

Printed and bound in China.